Dear Parent:

Congratulations! Your child is taking the first steps on an exciting journey. The destination? Independent reading!

STEP INTO READING® will help your child get there. The program offers five steps to reading success. Each step includes fun stories and colorful art. There are also Step into Reading Sticker Books, Step into Reading Math Readers, Step into Reading Phonics Readers, Step into Reading Write-In Readers, and Step into Reading Phonics Boxed Sets—a complete literacy program with something to interest every child.

Learning to Read, Step by Step!

Ready to Read   Preschool–Kindergarten
• big type and easy words • rhyme and rhythm • picture clues
For children who know the alphabet and are eager to begin reading.

Reading with Help   Preschool–Grade 1
• basic vocabulary • short sentences • simple stories
For children who recognize familiar words and sound out new words with help.

Reading on Your Own   Grades 1–3
• engaging characters • easy-to-follow plots • popular topics
For children who are ready to read on their own.

Reading Paragraphs   Grades 2–3
• challenging vocabulary • short paragraphs • exciting stories
For newly independent readers who read simple sentences with confidence.

Ready for Chapters   Grades 2–4
• chapters • longer paragraphs • full-color art
For children who want to take the plunge into chapter books but still like colorful pictures.

STEP INTO READING® is designed to give every child a successful reading experience. The grade levels are only guides. Children can progress through the steps at their own speed, developing confidence in their reading, no matter what their grade.

Remember, a lifetime love of reading starts with a single step!

*To Phyllis, with appreciation for the care
you've given to so many "Bootsies"
—M.B.*

*For Mom and Dad, Aaron and Josh
—P.C.*

ISBN 978-1-338-11022-7

Text copyright © 2011 by Maribeth Boelts.
Cover art and interior illustrations copyright © 2011 by Patricia Cantor.
All rights reserved. Published by Scholastic Inc., 557 Broadway, New York, NY 10012, by
arrangement with Random House Children's Books, a division of Penguin Random House LLC.
Step into Reading is a registered trademark of Penguin Random House LLC.
SCHOLASTIC and associated logos are trademarks and/or
registered trademarks of Scholastic Inc.

12 11 10 9 8 7 6 5 4 3 2 1   16 17 18 19 20 21

Printed in the U.S.A.   40

First Scholastic printing, September 2016

STEP INTO READING®

STEP 3

Sleeping Bootsie

by Maribeth Boelts

illustrated by Patricia Cantor

SCHOLASTIC INC.

Once upon a time,
there was a very lonely kitten.
She had nowhere to live.
Everyone shooed her away.

One day,

the kitten hid

in a laundry basket.

The basket was carried

into a castle.

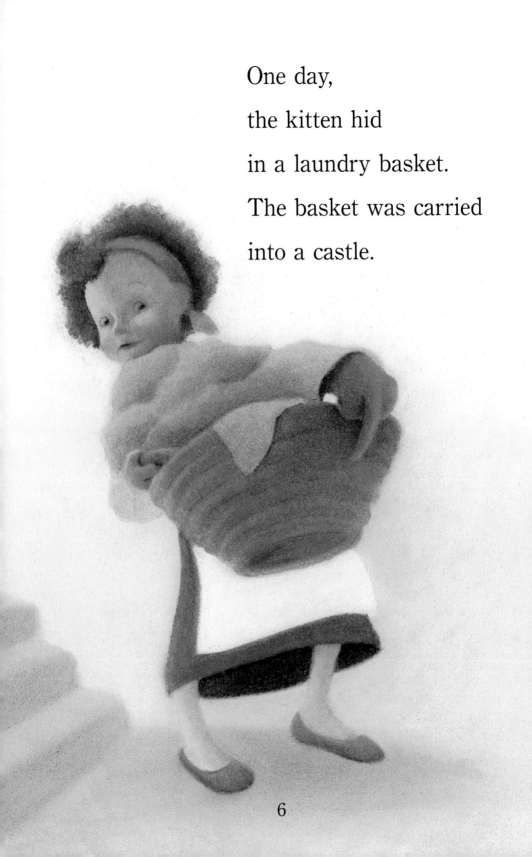

The kitten peeked from the basket.

She saw a maiden working hard.

The maiden washed and ironed

the royal family's clothes.

"I wish I had a friend,"

sighed the maiden.

The maiden saw something move
in the basket.
She looked inside.
It was a kitten!

The maiden placed the kitten

on her lap.

She petted the kitten.

The kitten purred and purred.

The maiden noticed

the kitten's white paws.

Her paws looked like boots.

"My name is Meg,"

said the maiden.

"If the queen lets me keep you,

I will name you Bootsie."

Meg had an idea.

She laid the queen's dress on her bed.

The queen put it on.

She found Bootsie in her pocket!

"Every castle needs a kitten,"
said the queen.
She turned to Meg.
"Will you take care of her?"
she asked.
Meg said yes!

The king and queen had a ball.
"Everyone can meet our new kitten,"
said the queen.
Three good fairies were invited
to the ball.

They each gave Bootsie a gift.

Pink Fairy waved her wand.

She made Bootsie playful.

Purple Fairy clicked her heels.

She gave Bootsie

a beautiful meow.

Yellow Fairy wiggled her nose.

"Your heart will always be kind."

Silver Fairy had not been invited.

Her magic was used for evil.

She came to the ball anyway.

Clap! Clap! Clap!

She cast her spell.

"You must not touch your paw

to water,"

said Silver Fairy.

"If you do,

you will fall into a deep sleep."

Silver Fairy said that

only one thing would wake Bootsie.

"What is it?"
cried Meg.
"Tell us!"
said the king and queen.

"She will wake only if she hears
her happiest sound,"
laughed Silver Fairy.

The king gave an order.

"Remove all water

from the castle!"

Guards drained the royal moat.

Maids emptied the royal hot tub.

"No baths allowed!"

said the king.

The dirty laundry piled up.

People fainted

when the royal family passed by.

The market sold out

of clothespins.

Bootsie couldn't leave the castle
because of the spell.
Everyone was busy keeping
water out of the castle.

No one could play.

Bootsie wandered sadly
from room to room.

Her beautiful meow disappeared.

One day,

a new maid came to work.

She snuck in

her pet goldfish.

She left her bedroom door open.

Bootsie crept in.

She hopped up

by the goldfish bowl.

Bootsie watched the goldfish
swim around.
Then she tapped her paw
on the water.

Bootsie dropped with a plop!

She fell into a deep sleep.

Meg found her.

"Oh, no!"

she cried.

Meg heard an evil laugh.

The new maid was Silver Fairy!

"Get out!"

Meg shouted.

The king and queen tried to wake
Sleeping Bootsie.
"Let's try some happy sounds,"
said Meg.
Singing birds filled the room.
Giggly children visited.

The royal marching band played.
The three good fairies
did magic.
They waved, clicked,
and wiggled.
But Sleeping Bootsie
slept and slept.

Meg stayed

by Sleeping Bootsie's side.

She brushed her fur.

She worried and waited.

One rainy night,
thunder boomed.
A wet stray kitten
looked for shelter.

"Go away!"

said the castle guard.

But the kitten crept back in
another way.
"Begone!"
scolded the cook.

But the kitten tried once more.

The little kitten searched

for someplace safe to sleep.

She found Meg

and Sleeping Bootsie.

The kitten crawled onto the bed.

She curled under the covers.

She purred and purred and purred.

Sleeping Bootsie's eyes opened!

She yawned.

She stretched.

She nuzzled Meg's cheek.

"Sleeping Bootsie, you're awake!"

said Meg.

"But what broke the spell?"

she wondered.

Then Meg heard soft purring.

She turned back the covers.

"Purrr,"

said the kitten.

"Purring is a cat's happiest sound!"
Meg exclaimed.

Sleeping Bootsie circled the kitten.

She licked the kitten's face.

"She needs a home, too,"

said Meg.

The king and queen said the kitten

could stay.

"Hooray!"

said Meg.

Sleeping Bootsie was

filled with joy.

She had Meg and a new friend.

Sleeping Bootsie began to meow.

Her beautiful meow was back!

Purple Fairy beamed.

The meow carried
through the kingdom.
Stray cats
stopped in their tracks.
Hungry kittens
came out of hiding.

Cats and kittens
dashed to the castle.
Sleeping Bootsie's kind heart
was a gift from Yellow Fairy.
Meg had a kind heart, too.

"We'll find homes for each of you,"
Meg promised.
"Meow!"
agreed Sleeping Bootsie.
It was happily ever after . . .
for everyone!